A very GOOD HELPER

Deanna Barnes

illustrated by **Joy Richardson**

Mynd Matters Publishing
715 Peachtree Street NE
Suites 100 & 200
Atlanta, GA 30308
www.myndmatterspublishing.com

978-1-953307-87-3 (PBK)
978-1-953307-88-0 (HDCV)

For my parents, Deborah and James

To my hearts, Brazley, Avery, Bennett and Greyson

— D.B.

For my parents, Barbara and Vincent

— J.R.

I don't know what my mom would do without me.

I help her make breakfast for the whole family.

I make sure my brothers and I are dressed in clothes that don't bore,

and that she gets healthy food from the store.

I help with chores to keep our house tidy and neat.

I make sure our yard is the prettiest on our street.

When I push the stroller, she never objects.

I lend a helping hand on all of the house projects.

I carefully fold and put away all of the laundry.

I am a chef when I help cook my favorite dinner—

RAVIOLI!

24

I help her wash dishes after we all dine,

and make sure the tub has bubbles for bath time.

She has no idea how tiring helping can be.

I don't know what my mom would do without me.